Greedy MacCready

written by
Julie Fulton

illustrated by
Jona Jung

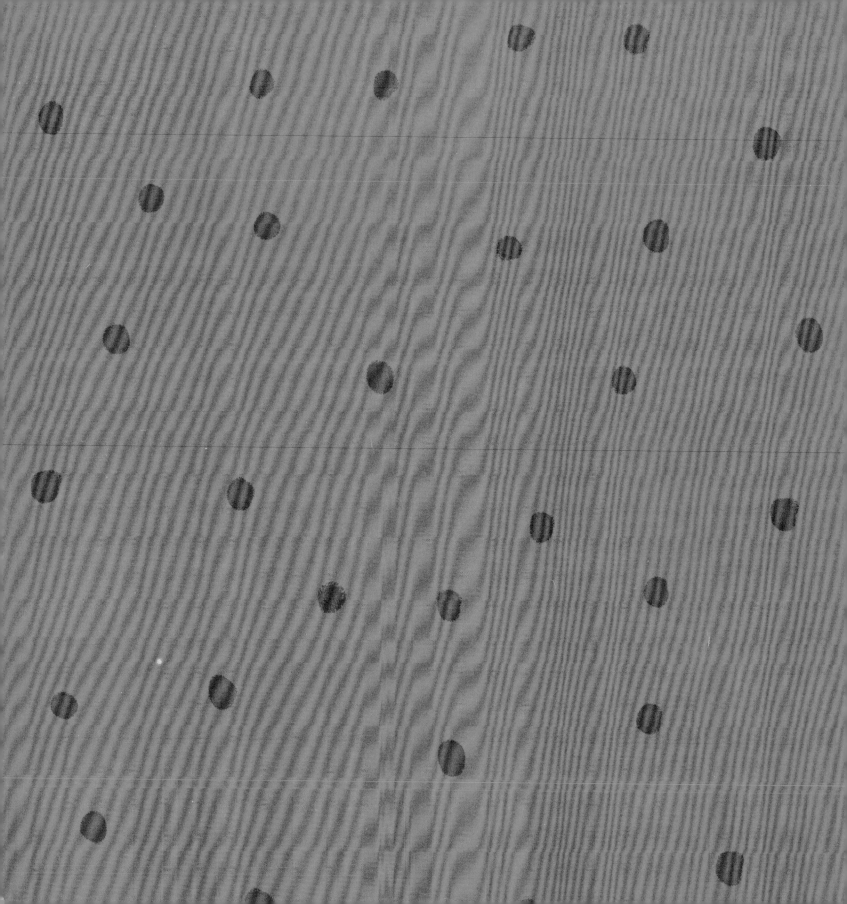

Mrs MacCready was ever so greedy
she did nothing else but eat.
Fish fingers and chips, apples with pips,
plates full of succulent meat.

Bacon and ham, gobbled with jam,
brown eggs scrambled or fried.
All sorts of berries, especially cherries
even with worms inside.

An indian curry she ate in a hurry
together with chutney and rice.
A pink **wobbly** jelly slid down to her belly,
followed by sweet sugar mice.

Hot spicy mustard and bright yellow custard,
a man made of warm gingerbread.
She loved his cute nose and sweet little toes,
but first she would **bite** off his head.

Roast potatoes and pork piled high on her fork
she popped in her mouth to chew,
with mushy green peas and smelly old cheese
she licked her plate clean, wouldn't you?

When in the right mood her **favourite** food
was chocolate cake covered in cream,
with strawberries on top and a big glass of pop.
It made all her neighbours scream.

"Mrs MacCready, you're far too greedy,
please find something else to do,
like play in the park or walk in the dark,
it's really much better for you."

But Mrs MacCready, ever so greedy
and certain that she knew best,
grew **bigger** and **bigger** 'til nothing would fit her
not even her fancy string vest.

The neighbours all tried to keep her inside,
hidden so no-one could see,
but a man from the paper heard of the caper
and printed the following plea...

...'A rather large lady from Hamilton Shady
needs something new to wear.
It has to be large, the size of a barge.
Do you have an item to spare?'

The readers were good and did what they could
sending her all sorts of stuff.
Trousers and shirts, jumpers and skirts,
but none of it quite big enough.

She was now such a height a balloon was too tight
and a parachute simply too small.
A wedding marquee decorated for free
was really just no good at all.

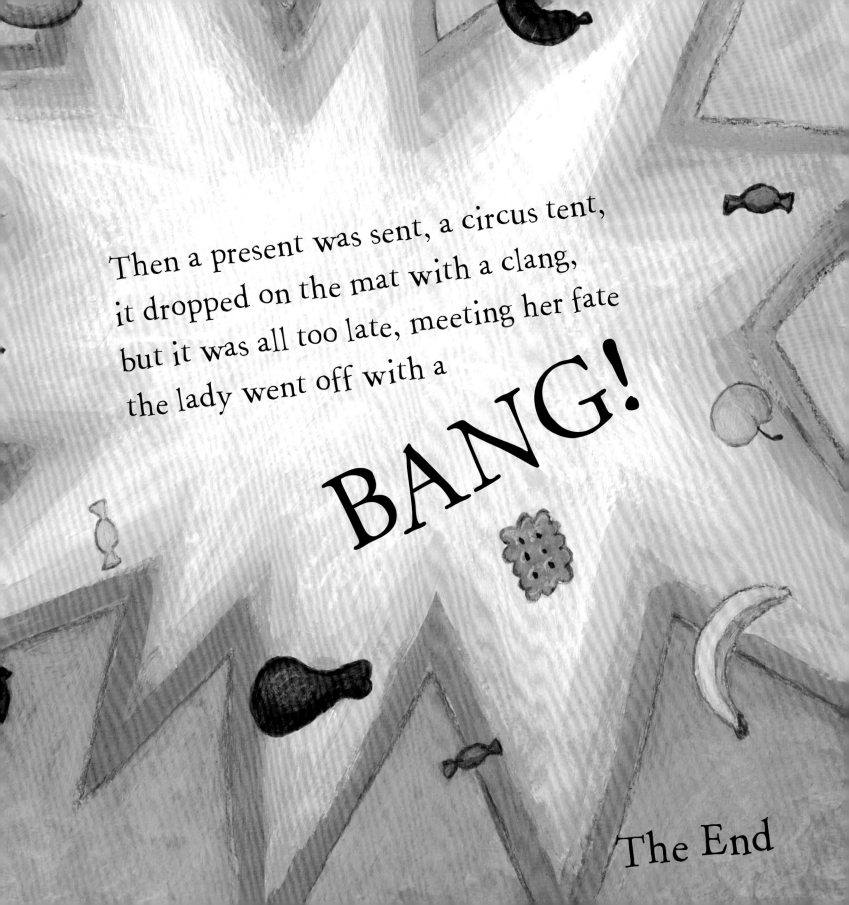

Then a present was sent, a circus tent,
it dropped on the mat with a clang,
but it was all too late, meeting her fate
the lady went off with a

BANG!

The End

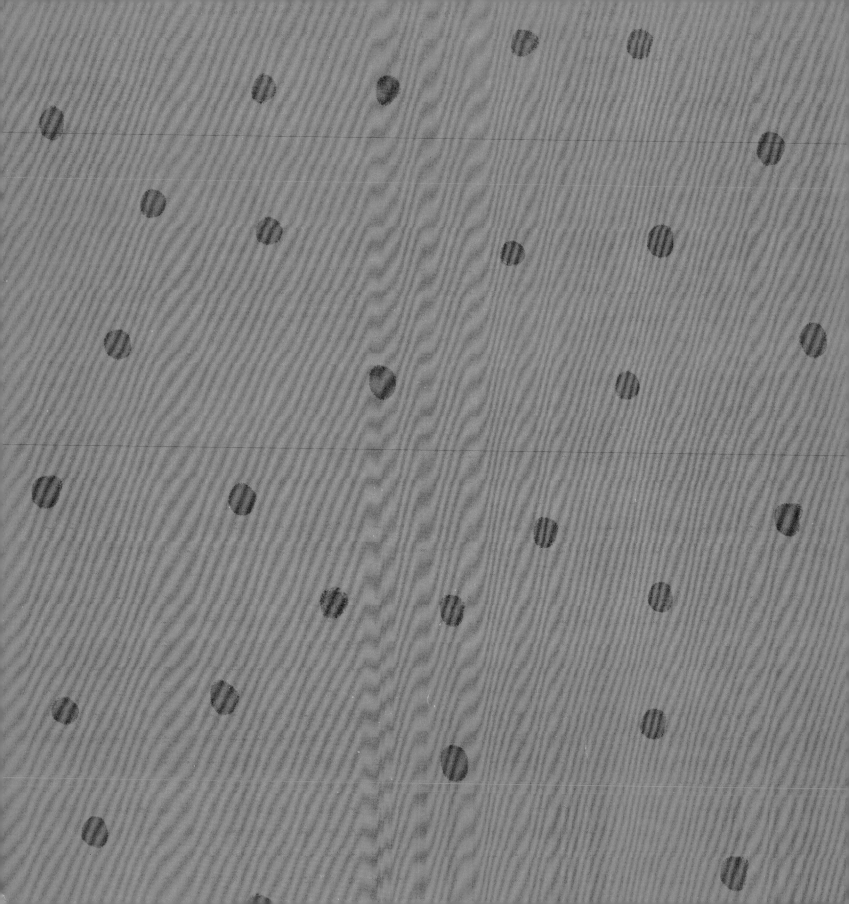

Greedy MacCready

An original concept by Julie Fulton

© Julie Fulton

Written by Julie Fulton

Illustrated by Jona Jung

Published by MAVERICK ARTS PUBLISHING LTD

Studio 3A, City Business Centre, 6 Brighton Road,

Horsham, West Sussex, RH13 5BB

+44 (0)1403 256941

© Maverick Arts Publishing Limited

Published March 2016

*A CIP catalogue record for this book is available
at the British Library.*

ISBN 978-1-84886-199-2

www.maverickbooks.co.uk